Digby's
Hollywood Story

Henry,
   Thanks very much
for including me in the
circulation of "Pie."
     Here's one of mine.
         Tom Luchs

Digby's Hollywood Story

Thomas Fuchs

Winchester, UK
Washington, USA

First published by Roundfire Books, 2015
Roundfire Books is an imprint of John Hunt Publishing Ltd., Laurel House, Station Approach,
Alresford, Hants, SO24 9JH, UK
office1@jhpbooks.net
www.johnhuntpublishing.com
www.roundfire-books.com

For distributor details and how to order please visit the 'Ordering' section on our website.

Text copyright: Thomas Fuchs 2014

ISBN: 978 1 78535 195 2
Library of Congress Control Number: 2015943102

A CIP catalogue record for this book is available from the British Library.

Design: Lee Nash

Printed in the USA by Edwards Brothers Malloy

We operate a distinctive and ethical publishing philosophy in all
areas of our business, from our global network of authors to
production and worldwide distribution.

Chapter 1

He wasn't frightened. He'd had a bad moment when it started, when he realized he'd been caught by a riptide, but he was an experienced swimmer. He knew what to do. Even as he was being pulled out farther and farther from the shore, he made the effort to relax. That's how people got killed, fighting against something so much stronger than themselves. He flipped over onto his back and floated. In a while, the current would weaken and then he would break free of it.

He had gone in for a late-afternoon swim, the sun near to setting. Now he saw the very moment that a band of high thin clouds turned a spectacular pink, and then the horizon flushed with the color, and then the sun was gone. It would be cold soon. More important than ever to stay calm.

After a while, he felt the power of the rip lessening, dissolving. He tried a few strokes, not against it but at a right angle to what was left of the flow. And now, he was free of it, free to swim back to shore. But where was that? A light fog had moved in, enough to obscure whatever moon- or star-light there might otherwise be. If he struck out for shore and was actually headed further out, toward nothing... Would he have to stay afloat until dawn? Could he do that?

Despite his determination to stay calm, emotion overcame him suddenly, a wave of sadness. This is what it came to? A chapter of his life had just closed, only months before, when the certain course of his life was changed by a miraculous and terrible event. He was stationed in Hawaii, destined to be part of the invasion of Japan. Then, out of nowhere, a super weapon, a single bomb destroys a city. Digby is saved. Six months later, he was a civilian, back in Santa Barbara working in a gas station and wondering what life held in store for him. And then he decided to go for a swim.

He knew he wouldn't die out here. That was just senseless, pointless. He pushed down the part of him that was reasonable, the part that knew there was little symmetry in a life and also knew how all stories, all real stories, ultimately end.

Then, as always happens if you don't die, there was a development. A glow appeared on the horizon, slight, flickering. The kind of light that might be from a bonfire on a beach.

He struck out for the glow, slowly, carefully, not an all-out effort. He had no way of knowing how far from shore he might be. It was crucial that he not exhaust himself before he made it.

He thought he could see figures now, in silhouette against the flames, moving around it. Was this an illusion...was he really getting that close? His body made the decision for him. He found himself in a strong crawl, deep, powerful strokes carrying him forward.

Suddenly, not far ahead, the froth of surf. He pushed on, more strokes, then dropped a leg and could just touch bottom. He kicked off, switching to a breaststroke, got closer still, dropped a leg again and found footing. He stood. The water was well below his thighs. He was able to walk out of the ocean and on to the beach, not twenty feet from the bonfire. He headed toward it and fell flat on his face.

The next thing he was aware of was that he was back on his feet, with a man at either side of him half holding him up and guiding him toward the fire. He had the impression that there were a lot of kids around, and some adults, and the smell of hot dogs.

A woman said, "He's freezing." Someone draped a beach towel around him; someone else handed him a cup of coffee. He sipped from it.

He had been saved by a kids' beach party, mainly girls but

some boys, most in their early teens, roasting hot dogs and marshmallows. There were a few adults with them, supervising, helping out.

"Thanks," said Digby to everyone and no one in particular.

One of the parents, a man, said, "You know, this is a private beach."

"I'm sorry," said Digby. "It was kind of a forced landing." One of the girls admonished him. "It's dangerous to go swimming in the dark."

"It wasn't dark when I started out," said Digby.

A man clutching a highball glass said, "Pretty snappy dialogue. You a writer?" He clearly thought himself a wit.

"No," said Digby. "I just went for a swim."

The man's wife chipped in. "An actor? You're not an actor, are you?" She and her husband snickered over this.

"No," said Digby.

"I ask," said the woman, "because actors go to really incredible lengths to get attention."

"I work in a gas station," said Digby. His relief and gratitude were turning to irritation. This was the strangest group of people he had ever fallen among. The riptide and the ordinary, underlying flow of the ocean had probably carried him well south of the place where he'd gone in.

"Exactly where am I?" he asked.

The woman who had said he was freezing spoke up. "Stop picking on the man," she said, and told Digby he was at the Malibu Colony.

Digby had heard of the Colony. It was where the Hollywood types with big money had their beach houses.

The woman asked if he was hungry. He nodded. She turned to one of the kids, saying, "Cindy..." and a nice-looking girl, a brunette on the verge of womanhood, pulled a stick from the fire with a charred hot dog bubbling and twisting on its end. She slid the dog off onto a bun and asked

Digby if he wanted mustard.

"No, no," he said. "That's fine. Thanks." He wolfed it down. By the time he finished, she had another one ready and he ate that, too. She was a good kid.

A man who had said nothing but had watched Digby closely through all this, now spoke up.

"What's your name, young man?" His attitude seemed to be that there had been enough fuss. It was time to get everything cleared up. He was, evidently, a man of some authority in this circle.

"Digby," said Digby. "Roger Digby, but everyone usually just calls me Digby."

The man nodded. "And how," he asked, "does it happen that you didn't know where you were?"

Digby told the story quickly, without much detail, finishing with, "So that's it. No mystery to it."

The man seemed satisfied. "Well," he said, "we'll have to get you back to where you went in. Your clothes are there?"

"I can hitch," said Digby.

"Come up to the house," said the man. "You'll need some clothes. Can you stand? You okay?"

Digby nodded. He and the man walked to a large, two-story brick home, one of a row of houses facing the beach, each of a different style, all of them substantial. No beach shacks here.

A garden hose was coiled near the front door. The man pointed to it, saying, "Rinse the sand off, would you? Sonya doesn't like sand in the house."

Sonya, evidently the man's wife, was close behind them. She turned out to be the woman who had asked if he was freezing and gotten the girl to feed him. Maybe some of these folks were a little strange, thought Digby, but they could also be decent.

After he had hosed off the sand, they brought him into the

house and directed him to an upstairs bedroom. "Take a nice hot shower," said the man. "We'll be in the living room."

When he was done with the shower and came out of the bathroom, he found clothes piled on a chair – a t-shirt, cotton pants, a pullover, and sandals. He dressed and went down to more coffee and more talk. The man drew him out with questions and expressions of interest. He and his wife seemed especially interested by his time in the service.

"I can't complain," said Digby. "I got off easy. A year, mostly in Hawaii." He laughed about being detailed to the M.P.s even though he had no background whatever in police work. "That's the Army for you. But I guess they know what they're doing. Anyway, I can't complain."

"And now?" asked the man. "Now, what are you planning to do with yourself?"

"I haven't decided," said Digby.

"Maybe go to college," said Sonya. "You've got the GI Bill."

Digby wondered why these people were chipping at him. "I've been going to school my whole life," he said, "and then right into the Army. I guess I just want some time to myself. See what comes along."

"Okay, okay," said the man. Sonya said nothing. Digby hoped he hadn't offended them. They obviously meant well. He stood up. "I'd better get going. I'll bring the clothes back tomorrow."

"Don't worry about that," said Sonya.

"And you don't have to hitch," said the man.

"No," said Digby. "I've been enough trouble."

"We've got a driver," said Sonya. "That's his job. He drives people."

"Kenny will take you," said the man. He went back outside. Through a window, Digby saw him signal to someone on the beach. He waited out there and when a young guy about Digby's age appeared, spoke to him. Then the two of them came back into the living room.

"This is Kenny," said the man. "Just tell him where you want to go." To Sonya he said, "It's getting cold out there. Maybe it's time for the kids to come in."

Digby said, "Thanks. You folks have been so kind."

In the car with Kenny, driving back up the coast road, Digby made some remark about how nice his hosts had been. It was only then that he realized that the man had never given his name.

Kenny laughed. "You don't know whose party you crashed?"

"No."

"Really? You don't? That's Mr. and Mrs. Vogler." When he saw the name meant nothing to Digby, he added, "Dave Vogler?" Still nothing from Digby, so he went on, "He owns a movie studio."

"No kidding?"

"No kidding," said Kenny. "And I've got news for you. Apparently you need a job?"

"Not really."

"You don't want to work at the studio? You should. It's a good life. Mr. Vogler said to tell you to report to the Personnel office at the studio any time this week. They'll be expecting you."

Digby had no idea what to make of this. He liked the movies well enough, but what could he do at a studio?

"They've got a lot of different jobs. And I gotta tell ya, Hollywood's a great place to meet women."

Before they got back to the beach where he had gone in for his swim, Digby learned a few more things from Kenny. The bonfire weenie roast was part of a birthday party for Cindy Vogler, their daughter. "The brunette with the bangs," said Kenny. That was the one who had given him the hot dogs.

Chapter 1

The Voglers had had another child, a son older than Cindy, named Jack. Jack hadn't come home from the war.

Chapter 2

The next day, while pumping gas and washing windshields, Digby mulled the whole thing over. Sometime in the middle of the afternoon, he thought to himself, *Maybe this is the beginning of the next chapter of my life*. The morning after that he drove down to L.A.

When he arrived at the main gate of the Vogler studio, a phone call by the cop on duty there confirmed that he was expected at the Personnel office. He parked as directed in a Visitor's slot and set out on foot, guided by a paper map with the route marked out on it by the guard. The studio was a labyrinth of stages, workshops and office buildings laid out over roughly the equivalent of four city blocks. As he made his way across it, he was impressed by the calm energy of the place and by the casual juxtaposition of the matter-of-fact and the fantastic. A small group of women in filmy harem pants and billowy tops strolled past him, followed shortly by a man in armor on a horse. A powerful car with its blinds drawn pulled up nearby. No one got in or out. He passed a parked flatbed truck, carrying a cage with a great shaggy lump on its floor that turned out on closer examination to be a sleeping bear. The studio looked like it might be an interesting place to work.

At the Personnel office, he had to wait only a few minutes before he was sent in to see a Mr. Bowers, a nice enough old guy who, after fifteen minutes or so of question and answer, leaned back in his swivel chair and said, "You know something about cars and something about police work. You're not worth a fight with the Teamsters, so I think Chief Lou's the place for you. I'll let him know you're coming."

"Chief Lou?" asked Digby.

"Studio police. You should fit in fine there." He directed

Digby down a corridor, across a courtyard, then down another corridor to a door with a plaque: *Louis G. Bullard, Chief.* He knocked and was told to come in.

The chief was a lean, wiry man, maybe approaching fifty but still fit. "M.P.s, huh?" he said, without any preamble.

"Yes, sir."

"You're not in the Army anymore. Just call me Lou."

Digby nodded.

"Okay," said Lou, and then laid it all out. As a member of the force, Digby's duties would consist mainly of helping to manage parking, manning the drive-on and walk-on gates, and patrolling the premises to ensure that no unauthorized people got on to the lot. Digby thought he ought to ask about the pay.

"You thinking of turning me down?" asked Lou. He was smiling but there was – what was it, exactly, disbelief, anger? Evidently, Lou didn't regard himself as someone you said no to. Then he said, "The pay is seventy bucks a week. That okay with you?"

It was very much okay, almost twice what he was making at the station. "It's great!" said Digby. "Thanks."

"Okay, then," said Lou. "Go back to Personnel, fill out the forms, then come back here and we'll get you into the schedule."

As he was leaving, Digby asked how to get to Mr. Vogler's office.

"What do you want to know that for?"

"I want to thank him."

"No need," said Lou. "He'll know you're hired and he'll know you're grateful."

Digby became the newest of a force of sixteen, most of them slow, deliberate men in their fifties. He was aware that he stood out among them, a young veteran, alert and eager to do well. It wasn't long before he had his duties down. Patrolling

10

like a cop with a city beat – sometimes on foot, sometimes on a bike or in one of the studio's electric golf carts – he learned the neighborhood and its routines A flashing red light outside one of the cavernous, hangar-like stages wasn't cause for alarm, only a signal that a take was in progress and no one should enter. The sweet smell of freshly cut pine scraps in a bin outside the wood shop meant carpenters were busy building new sets. A phrase of piano music repeated over and over, floating out an open window somewhere, meant a composer was at hard at work.

The Vogler studio lacked the acres of backlot attached to the largest studios, like MGM and Fox, for the shooting of exteriors but it did have a few standing outdoor sets, including a city street and a Western street, storefronts with no insides.

To help insure that all its various workers stayed on the lot and at or near their tasks, the studio provided much that they might seek outside, including a barbershop, a dry cleaner and two restaurants: one a café, the other a full-service operation.

As part of the scheme to keep employees close at hand, the studio allowed the peddlers of various good and services to circulate on the lot. There was Fred Diamond, who peddled jewelry and Henry Stoll, who sold insurance. Maury Katz wheeled his clothing rack from building to building, offering shirts and ties, excellent quality, good prices. All were soon known to Digby as was he to them.

He and George Marcus had a little morning routine going. Whenever he saw Marcus pulling into his privileged parking spot close to the main Administration building, he would say, "Morning, Mr. Marcus," and Marcus would respond with, "Hiya, kid. What do you like?"

Digby's answer was always the same, "I'm not a player today, Mr. Marcus," Marcus finishing the routine with, "Just as well, kid. just as well." Marcus was the studio bookie.

There were plenty of actors and actresses, many of the category "looks familiar but the name…", others instantly recognizable. Sometimes, it was the voice as much as anything, as on the afternoon a man came up alongside Digby and asked, "Say, pal, you got a light?" Digby knew it was Bogart even before he turned to look.

Jack Scott looked exactly as he did on screen, except that he was a lot smaller. Digby saw him shoot a scene in which he stood on a box so it wouldn't be apparent to audiences that his leading lady was taller than him.

Few of the women were anywhere near as sexy in person as they were in their movies. There were exceptions. Digby's heart beat and he grew hard the first time he saw Ava Gardner; the two-dimensional, black and white image even more erotic as living flesh.

Without any effort or particular desire, Digby was learning a little about movie making. A long day of tedious effort on a stage, the positioning and repositioning of cumbersome equipment – the camera, the lights and mikes – to get a shot and then a bead of sweat running down an actress's lip meant the shot had to be done again. One day, he watched Barbara Stanwyck lying on a bed, a massive platform positioned just inches above her bearing the weight of a camera, the cameraman and the director. Clever lighting made her hair glow. She reached out, welcoming the camera as a lover. After several takes, the director was satisfied, "Cut. Print it." The platform was moved. Stanwyck got out of the bed. A lady from Wardrobe handed her a dressing gown, a man from Make Up did something to her face and she moved on to the set-up for the next shot. Digby was struck by how something that would flow seamlessly on the screen had to be so painstakingly constructed.

His education was further advanced one morning when he was on patrol. He was passing the nursery, a patch thick with potted greens, mainly bushes and small trees, some real, many artificial, stored here for use as set dressing when needed. Just inside the perimeter of this jungle, a man wearing a tweed jacket and a tie sat on a folding chair, smoking a cigarette. The tie and jacket meant that he probably wasn't a greensman or crew member. He was out of place.

Digby called out, "Hello. You in there."

The man, still seated, turned slowly toward Digby, as though coming out of a reverie. "Me?" he asked. "You mean me?"

Digby got out of his cart. The man came out of the little jungle. He was someone Digby had seen somewhere before but couldn't place . Not an actor. And he didn't have the self-assurance Digby usually sensed in directors, or the assertive bearing of most producers.

"Is everything all right?" asked Digby.

The man looked at him for a beat and then said, "Well, I do have a problem."

Oh, thought Digby, *a nervous-breakdown case.* He'd heard about these creative types having mental and emotional problems. But who was he? There was something familiar about him. Digby was reluctant to ask his name. Most of the people on the lot thought themselves important enough to be well known, and many were. It was part of his job to avoid giving offense.

"I like to get out of my office sometimes, when I have a problem I'm working on," said the man.

"Anything I can do to help?"

The man smiled a smile of condescension. "It's a story problem," he said. "I'm a writer. Alan Swink."

"Yes, of course, Mr. Swink," said Digby.

"Say, wait a minute," said Swink. "You're that guy... Are you? Sure, you're the guy who got in the riptide?"

That's it, thought Digby. This guy and his wife were the

couple that razzed him when he came out of the water at Vogler's beach party. He nodded to Swink and said, amiably enough, "That's me, all right. Your wife thought I was an actor."

"You did make a hell of an entrance," said Swink. "And here you are… How are you getting on? You work here now?"

"I do," said Digby, "and I like it fine."

The writers had a building to themselves that Digby thought very pleasant. It looked like a large house of a kind he imagined they had in England – plaster, wood beams, shingled, with an old shade tree, a courtyard and even a fountain – but it wasn't unknown for them to be found wandering around the lot. It must be very boring, sitting by yourself in front of a typewriter hour after hour.

"What's the problem?" asked Digby. "You said you have a problem."

"I'm stuck," said Swink. "The studio bought this story, it was in *Collier's*. It's a short-short, about a detective who has to solve a series of murders. The gimmick is, he finds out at the end that he's the one doing the killing."

"I don't get it," said Digby.

"He's nuts," said Swink. "He's a looney."

"Oh, I see," said Digby. "Very good, very clever."

"It sounds great, it's a great short-short, probably gonna be a classic, but try doing it for nine reels, it gets pretty thin. So I suggested that it isn't him, really. He has a twin brother."

"And his twin's the killer?"

"But he doesn't know he has a twin. Their parents died when they were babies and they got sent off to different foster homes."

"It gets a little complicated," said Digby.

"You're telling me," said Swink. "I wish I'd kept my mouth shut and then someone else would be stuck with this. Though I have to say, in a way the gimmick pictures are easier than ones that are supposed to be realistic. How do you make something so contrived as a story seem realistic?" He sighed, sucked on his cigarette, then, smiling, playing off the old joke, he added, "Plots. Can't live with them, can't live without them."

Like most people, Digby assumed, without ever thinking about it, that the characters in a movie got into situations, reacted, said things to one another just the way they do in real life, that there isn't much difference between a story and the natural unfolding of events. But now that he thought about it, of course, someone had to make it up.

Swink looked at his watch and asked, "Do you happen to know if George Marcus is on the lot?"

"He is," said Digby. "As a matter of fact, I saw him pull in about fifteen minutes ago. Come on, I'll give you a lift."

"Um, um, well... Thanks anyway, but I'll just finish my cigarette, if you don't mind," said Swink and back he went to his place in the jungle.

Chapter 3

When Digby told Kenny, the Vogler chauffeur, about his encounter with Swink, the thing Kenny found most interesting was how he seemed to be avoiding the bookie. He said, "That Marcus is a smooth operator but tough, very tough."

"A break-your-legs kind of guy?" asked Digby.

"Could be," said Kenny. "At least he wants people to think so. That way, they don't fool around and pay him when they owe him."

Kenny was on the lot almost every day, what with driving Mr. Vogler and running errands. Most of the time when he and Digby chatted, it was about women, mainly where and how to meet them. Kenny was full of advice. He was enthusiastic about what he called "the three Bs".

"Which are?" asked Digby.

"Bars, of course," said Kenny, "and the beach, when then weather's good and…" – a dramatic pause – "bowling alleys."

"Bowling alleys?"

"Yep," said Kenny. "It's a very social sport. There's always something to start a conversation about. Congratulate 'em on a good score. Offer advice – 'You might want to try the ten-pound ball'… 'You're twisting your hip. Here, let me put my hands there so you can see...'" He grinned, adding, "And sometimes you get two Bs for one because some bowling alleys have bars." He rattled off a few of his favorites.

"Thanks for the info," said Digby. "My problem's been what to do with them once I meet 'em."

"Well, son…" said Kenny.

Digby explained. He was living in a cheap residential hotel that was not far from the studio but was cramped, hot and frequently noisy. Certainly not a place he'd want to bring a girl to. He'd left his name at a new place that had a vacancy coming up.

"Yeah?" said Kenny. "Where's it at?"

"In the County strip, just below Sunset. It's one of those courtyard set-ups, you know, where the apartments are all around a courtyard. Nice. It's called Las Casitas des Artistes." The name was written in broad strokes on a sign shaped like a painter's palette. Digby thought the women might like it but Kenny shook his head.

"No, no," he said. "You're forgetting the privacy factor. In one of those places, because of the courtyard, because you gotta walk through that, there's no privacy. Everyone knows all the time who's coming and going. You don't want that. You want to be in a place like I'm in."

"I sort of thought you lived at the Voglers'."

"Yeah, there's a little place over the garage and I'm there a lot but I've got an apartment in a swell building off Vine. Underground parking, then into the elevator, which is self-service and you're home."

"But people see you anyway," said Digby.

"Not so much as in a courtyard, and the whole attitude's different. It's more like a hotel. Everyone minds their business. Let me look around. I'll find something."

About a week later, he did. "Hey, Digby, there's a vacancy in my building." He and Kenny became neighbors, though they lived on different floors.

Digby already knew about bars and the beach. He tried bowling alleys a couple of times but didn't have much luck. He did better at the Fleur Des Lis, a quiet little bar on La Brea, and there was Tom Bergin's on Fairfax, with a dining room in the back, and the Frolic Room, a not-so-nice bar at the not-so-nice eastern edge of Hollywood, where he met a few girls who were quite nice.

Most of these encounters, pleasant as they were in the moment, led to nothing; others to involvements that were intense but brief. There was Anna, the redhead who believed in reincarnation and became certain she and Digby had been lovers in a former life. Several former lives, in fact. Usually in these prior lives, both of them were people of consequence, kings and queens. Her stories about what had happened in these past existences were illuminated with considerable color and detail. Some of them did seem vaguely familiar to Digby. Could there be anything to it, to reincarnation? Then he realized that one of the past lives sounded a lot like a movie he'd seen when he was a kid. He had been looking forward to it as an adventure with lots of action and fighting because the poster showed Errol Flynn posed with an upraised sword. He was bitterly disappointed when he paid his fifteen cents only to sit through a love story about Queen Elizabeth. He suspected that all of Anna's past lives were regurgitated movie plots but continued to find her diverting until he realized that she wasn't just kidding around. She really believed in what she was saying. Thereafter Digby avoided her.

Then there was the morning that he pulled up at a stoplight at Sunset and Gower and a woman he didn't know, had never seen her before, stepped from the curb, opened the passenger door, slid in next to him, and said, "Take me to the ocean."

She didn't look crazy or dangerous. Young. Nineteen or twenty. Nice build. Blonde, green eyes.

The light changed. In the moment when Digby was deciding whether to continue on or pull over and dump her out, she explained, "I've been in this town for two weeks and I haven't seen the ocean."

"Okay," said Digby, "let's go to the beach." He slid the car into gear and headed west. He had the morning off, had been planning to go to the Roosevelt pool but this promised to be interesting.

It was stop and go through Hollywood. At the next light, he asked her where she was from.

"Hays, Kansas."

"Seen many of the sights?"

"No."

He tried again. "Are you just visiting?"

"What do you mean?"

"I mean are you going to go back in a while?"

"No." she said. "Have you ever been to western Kansas?"

"No."

"There's not much there," she said.

"Oh. My name's Digby, by the way."

"I'm Joan."

"Nice to meet you."

"You, too," she said.

Silence.

To get things going again. Digby asked if she had ideas about what she might do in Los Angeles. "If you don't mind my asking?" he added.

She shrugged. "I don't mind. I'm gonna get a job at one of the department stores. Selling. The best stores are Saks, Bullocks, Robinsons. I've applied there."

Digby was impressed. As far as he could remember, this was the first good-looking girl, newly arrived, who didn't think she might have a chance in pictures.

They were through Hollywood and in the County strip. He pointed out the nightclubs as they passed them, Ciro's, Mocambo, the Troc. "Nothing going on now, of course," he said, "but at night, they jump."

"I'll keep that in mind," she said. The way she said this made Digby think she was high-hatting him, suggesting she was above going to clubs. Maybe it would have been better to have kicked her out of his car when she got in. But he felt he was committed now to taking her to the beach, and he was curious to see what her reaction would be the first time she saw the mighty Pacific. That ought to change her attitude.

They were past Doheny, running through Beverly Hills, the section with the wide median strip that was used as a bridal path. A rider wearing a red English hunting jacket appeared, trotting toward them at a pretty good clip. As they passed, he smiled and waved. It was Cary Grant. Was it just a general good-natured wave or did he remember Digby? Grant had done a picture for the studio and Digby had parked his car for the star a number of times. In the movies, Grant was almost always smooth, reserved – people came to him. In person, he seemed unsettled, almost anxious, reaching out, wanting to be liked. Now, between Grant's speed and the speed of the car, they passed each other so quickly Digby didn't have a chance to wave back. He hoped Grant wouldn't be offended.

"I think that was Cary Grant," he said.

"Yeah, you think so?" she said. "He looked familiar to me."

He didn't bother to tell her that they were in Beverly Hills or that they were passing the Beverly Hills Hotel rising up, pink and green, from the stands of palms surrounding it.

He pushed the car up the slope climbing out of the western edge of Beverly and into the winding stretch past UCLA and Bel Air. "Turn on the radio, if you want," he said.

"Nah," she said. "I'm fine."

The road straightened out again, carrying them through the village of Pacific Palisades, then more curves. Any moment now, yes, there…through the trees lining the road, the first glimpse of the sea. What would she say when she saw it? Another turn and the view was gone. She'd missed it.

A turn and another view of the water. Still no reaction. Did she see it and not realize what she was seeing? The ocean and the sky were almost exactly the same color at that moment, maybe she thought the ocean was just a continuation of the sky.

But then they were on the final downslope, almost like a plane coming in for a landing. What lay before them was unmistakable, the strip of the Coast Highway, the sand, the surf, the waves, the great, great, endless ocean. She said nothing. Probably speechless.

"Well?" asked Digby.

"So that's it," was all she said.

Digby was baffled, and angry. *It's the goddamned Pacific Ocean, the biggest ocean in the world. Who the hell is this dame, anyway? I drove her all the way out here for this?* But then his inherent good nature took over and he thought, *Well, she still doesn't get it.*

When they got down to the intersection with the coast road, he made a right, heading north. He'd take her up to that place near Trancas, where they could get sandwiches and beer and walk on the beach, but when they got there, the place was closed. He remembered that it was only open on weekdays during the summer.

He pulled across the road, parked at the edge of the sand. "Come on," he said to her. "Take off your shoes."

He led her down to where the sand was wet and easy to walk on. They went along for a while, skirting the waves as they lapped in and drew out. There was a light breeze off the water, gentle and fresh. "Well," he asked her, "now, what do you think?"

She looked out over the water and to his astonishment said, "It's just another kind of empty, only it's water instead of dirt. I'm sick of emptiness."

"Come on," said Digby. "I'll take you back."

"Look," she said, "don't get me wrong. Thanks for bringing me out here. I wanted to see it. Now I have. I just thought there'd be something more dramatic."

Neither of them said much as Digby drove them back into

town. Because of the awareness Digby was beginning to develop about the mechanics of movie making, how pictures were conceived and made, he sometimes found himself thinking how much easier some things, like this ride back to town would be in a movie. It would be compressed to a maybe half a minute. With the way they edited it, the different angles and the close ups and maybe some music, there would be the mood, the awkwardness, without the audience having to sit through the whole forty minutes and more this was taking.

After they had passed through Beverly Hills again and were back in Hollywood, Digby asked her where she wanted to be dropped.

"If it's not too far out of your way, on Lodi Place. Do you know where that is?"

"Sure," said Digby. He didn't ask her where on Lodi. It was a funny little street, just two short blocks running between Fountain and Santa Monica. A few minutes later, he was turning on to it. She pointed ahead. "Just up there," she said.

She was pointing to the Studio Club, which, as Digby knew, was a kind of supervised dormitory for young actresses, working and would-be.

"I thought you were looking for a sales job," said Digby.

The lady he knew as Joan, smiled and suddenly seemed a different person. "I lied," she said. "I hope you'll forgive me. I'm under contract at Fox."

"I don't get it," said Digby.

"I'm preparing for a part. It was an exercise. My coach told me to go out in public as Joan Morgan, to be Joan Morgan, to engage with people that way. She's kind of a pill. That's the thing about her character. She's an 'I've-seen-it-all' kind of a kid."

Jesus, thought Digby. *What a goddamned waste of time.* "So you're name's not Joan," said Digby, "and I suppose you're not really from Kansas and you've probably seen the ocean before."

"You're sore?"

"Yeah," said Digby, "to tell you the truth."

"It got out of hand. I'm sorry. You've been really nice. I'm sorry."

"It was kind of a dirty trick," said Digby. He felt himself cooling down. She seemed sincere, although…

She was going on, "I'm really from Long Beach. My name is Betsy MacDougal. My real name. On the screen I'll be Elizabeth Mackenzie. They thought MacDougal sounded funny. A good name for a comedienne maybe, but I'm not a comedienne."

"No, you're not," said Digby.

She got out of the car. "You've been a good sport."

"Yeah," said Digby. He found himself just interested enough to want to get at her a little. "You know, if you ever try that again, you might get in with the wrong guy."

"Oh," she said. "You looked safe. Besides, I figured if anything went wrong, I could always scream my head off."

Digby was still wondering about 'you looked safe' when she added, "You know, you should be careful who you pick up. Some girls can be trouble."

"I didn't have much choice," said Digby. Then he added, "Besides, I figured I could always scream my head off." It wasn't a great comeback, but it would have to do. He put the car into gear and drove off, wondering – if this whole thing had been in a movie, would it be a thriller, a mystery, a romance? Maybe it was a comedy and he was the chump.

There was still time for his original destination, the pool at the Hollywood Roosevelt. After a couple of laps he found he still had Betsy MacDougal or whatever the hell her name was on his mind. He called the Studio Club and got the operator to put him through.

Chapter 3

When she came on the line, he said, "This is Digby, the guy who took you to..."

She cut him off with, "I know who are." She said it with a smile in her voice, so he went ahead and asked her if he could take her out for a drink that evening.

"Okay," she said. "Sure."

He took her to D'Amico's, with its linoleum floor and world-weary waiters, because it wasn't a favorite, not a place he usually went to. He didn't particularly want to run into any of the women he might meet at his regular spots.

They were barely started on their first round when she asked him what he did for a living. He'd been down this road before. When he told a girl he worked at the studio, her eyes brightened; when he told her what he did, the light dimmed. When he told Betsy, she said, "Sounds like it might be interesting work." They went on to a second round and then dinner.

They found enough to talk about – where they came from, what they did with their time, how and why they'd come to Hollywood. Digby had told the story of his emergence from the sea a number of times and had gotten pretty good at it.

"I wish I'd been there to see it," she said. "You coming out of the ocean, like Sinbad or something."

"You make it sound like a movie when you say it like that," said Digby.

Betsy told her story. She had always loved the movies and from about as far back as she could remember, she had wanted to be an actress. She'd worked at it as she could, appearing in local beauty pageants and modeling for newspaper ads. One of the advertisers was a car dealer, who one day sold a car to a man at Fox. She got the car man to get the Fox man to see her. He, in turn, had been impressed and arranged a screen test. The results were judged promising enough for her to be signed to a talent-development contract.

It wasn't uncommon for the studios to pick up people who seemed promising and train them. Fox was giving Betsy acting lessons, singing lessons, dancing lessons, and paying her. The contract obligated her for seven years, while the studio could drop her at any time. Most of the kids going this route wouldn't amount to much and would be gone in a year or less. Every once in a while, one proved valuable. Betsy was determined to be one of those of who broke through and got herself a career.

At the end of the meal, Digby asked her if she wanted to go for a drive.

"Back to the beach?" she asked, smiling.

Digby laughed. "No, not that again."

"Maybe I just want to go home," she said.

He didn't think she did. "Do you?"

"No."

Digby decided it was worth a try. He was right. When he said, "What I'd really like to do is take you to my place." She said okay.

Betsy proved to be a practical girl who wasn't shy about letting Digby know what she wanted and finding out what pleased him. He took her back to the Studio Club late that night but thereafter, she frequently stayed until morning. When she did, they usually had coffee and a little breakfast together in the kitchen. He liked just sitting at the table as she moved around the room wearing a wrap that came down to her thighs, her legs long and creamy. She thought them a little too long. He thought they were perfect.

One morning, while he was in the kitchen and Betsy was still in bed, a dog outside he'd never heard before began sounding off, deep barks in a rapid series, and then a rumbling-rattling was rushing toward him. The floor pitched like the deck of a boat hit hard by a wave. He turned, headed for the bedroom, and had to catch at the counter to keep from falling. And then it was over and everything was still.

"Betsy, Betsy," he called as he went, to find her sitting up in bed.

"That was a doozy," she said.

"That was an earthquake," said Digby.

"So I noticed. Your first?"

"No," he said. "We have them in Santa Barbara, too, you know."

Out in the hallway, doors were opening and closing, the voices of neighbors rose. Someone called, "Hurry, hurry." Someone else said something about not panicking. Digby asked Betsy if she wanted to get out of the building.

"The first shock is usually the worst, isn't it?" she said. "If the roof hasn't collapsed by now... I've been in worse." Then she said, "Weren't you going to get me some coffee?"

What an amazing woman. He liked her so much. He admired her. He wanted to protect her. But she didn't seem to need a protector.

There were no promises, they made no plans, there was no talk of the future. Digby looked forward to the times he would be seeing her, saved up stories of funny or odd things that happened at work, passed along bits of gossip he thought might be interesting or useful to her. He found himself looking at jewelry displayed in shop windows, wondering which she would like, if he could afford such gifts.

Her work at Fox kept her busy. She didn't always return the calls he left for her at the Studio Club switchboard. Days, a week, might go by without his seeing or even speaking to her. The first time he complained about this, she explained in some detail what it was that had taken up her time, the preparation for a particular audition. Thereafter, her explanations were shorter and she became visibly exasperated and then they were at the point where her answer was no more than a look that said, "I've told you. I get busy."

It occurred to Digby that he might have a rival. When he mentioned this in one of his chats with Kenny, his friend advised him to see other women. "They're out there, man, all over this town." Digby knew this was so but none of the ones he'd met were anywhere near as interesting, as sexy, as confident or as much fun as Betsy.

She was almost always more or less on his mind. She was the first thing he thought of the night he was awakened by the building security buzzer. He stumbled out of the bedroom, to the intercom.

"Hello?"

But it was Lou. "Let me in."

"Yeah, sure," said Digby. He wondered what was up. Lou had never come by before. He pulled on a robe and waited. Minutes passed, more than enough time for Lou to get to his place. He opened the door, looked down the hall. Maybe Lou had gone to the wrong apartment. He left the door half open, got a beer from the kitchen, drank it slowly sitting in the living room. After half an hour, he closed the door and went back to bed. The next morning, at work, he asked Lou what happened to him.

"I did what I came to do and then I left. Sorry about waking you."

"You never came up."

"I saw who I came to see." He picked up a copy of the *Racing Form* and a pencil and lost himself in a study of the day's possibilities.

About a week passed before Digby realized he hadn't seen Kenny on the lot or around the building. After another week or so, the building manager stopped him in the lobby.

"You wouldn't," he asked, "have any idea what's happened to Ken Masters?"

"I don't know that anything has happened," said Digby.

"He's gone," said the manager. "Didn't pay his rent this

month."

"Did you try his work? They might be keeping him busy. You know, he drives for Dave Vogler. He stays over there."

"He doesn't work there anymore. I have that number. I called."

"I don't know," said Digby. "I really don't."

"His closets and drawers are empty, but he left some furniture," said the manager. "If you want any of it, I'll sell it to you. Cheap."

The next day, Digby told Lou all this.

"Yeah," said Lou. "I heard something about that. I know you guys were friends. You won't be seeing him around."

"What happened?"

"The guy was a dope," said Lou. "A real dope. You know what the dumb sonofabitch did? He put the moves on the Vogler kid, their girl, Cindy. Dumb sonofabitch."

Oh, Jesus, thought Digby. *What did Lou do that night?* Later, he remembered that the manager had said that Kenny had taken his clothes. So he probably wasn't lying off the Santa Monica pier or in a ditch somewhere.

When he told Betsy about it, she shivered visibly and said, "I wouldn't go poking my nose any deeper into that."

"Don't worry," said Digby.

"You know, know only what you're supposed to know and you'll be fine."

Then she broke the news to him about the change in her life. She was leaving the Studio Club, moving in to her own place, a nice apartment on Spaulding, just below Wilshire, in Beverly Hills. She was able to this because she'd gotten a raise. She'd gotten the raise because she was, finally, cast in part greater than a few lines. It was to be a comedy, with John Payne. She'd be busy, very busy. This would probably be their last time together for a while.

"Okay," said Digby. "I'm glad you got the picture. Okay."

That's how it was in this town. That's how it was with women like Betsy. They were here for a reason and it wasn't to meet men like him. He'd just have to forget about her. He'd have to. But how do you make yourself forget someone?

Chapter 4

As part of an effort to put Betsy behind him, Digby asked Lou for as much overtime work as possible, which was how he wound up on the location shoot for a picture the studio was making called *Dark Horizon*. The director had decided to film his exteriors – his street scenes – on real city streets rather than use the studio's street set.

The movie was about a pair of doomed lovers and a bungled hold up, set in a grimy world of small-time crooks and gamblers. Location scouts had found an appropriate setting for some of the action in the Pico Union District just below and to the west of downtown, crowded, worn and gray.

It struck Digby as odd that going off the lot and into the real world to shoot meant turning the real world into a movie set. The camera required cranes and dollies to make its moves, and there was all the other equipment: lights and reflectors, portable generators, multiple lines of thick black cable snaking everywhere underfoot. And of course there were the trucks for hauling all this, as well as trailers for Make Up, catering, dressing rooms. This all required guarding. Digby was one of the guards, outfitted in the standard studio-cop uniform, complete with visor cap, Sam Browne belt and badge. No holster, no gun.

It was the second day of the shoot and the company was already a half day behind schedule. Everyone was on edge. A complicated tracking shot featuring one of the stars, the single-named Veronique, a recent discovery brought over from France, kept going wrong, to the vast and obvious annoyance of the director.

Finally, he was satisfied and Veronique was free to return to her trailer. After a few moments there, she came back out and started off, away from the location. No one noticed her go, except Digby, who followed after her. Maybe, being from France, she didn't realize what a bad neighborhood this was.

He didn't know what to call her. 'Veronique' seemed too familiar. He didn't know her last name. Miss? No, wait, Mademoiselle, was that right? He settled on Madame and called that out to her as he caught up with her. "Madame, is there something you need? Can I help you?"

She stopped, turned, looked at him, and said in a low voice with a French accent, "Very kind of you but what I need is a little time to myself."

Digby was undeterred. "I won't bother you. I'll just walk along. It's a rough neighborhood. Pretend I'm not here."

She softened. "You are a gallant one," she said and allowed him to walk with her. "Do you think there is some shop along here where I can buy cigarettes?"

"I'm sure there is," said Digby. She was a small woman, nothing extraordinary about her appearance. He wondered vaguely, *Why her?* What about her made her so striking on film that the studio had gone to the great trouble and expense of bringing her over? He wondered if Betsy would prove to have that magical quality.

As they crossed to the next block, he saw with relief that they wouldn't have to go much further from the set. "There," he said, "the liquor store. You can get cigarettes there."

They drew closer, were almost at the store when a man came out, walking in their direction. The brim of his hat was pulled low, his face turned downward. He glanced up, seemed startled by the sight of them, turned and headed away, not back from where he'd come but off the sidewalk and across the street.

Digby took Veronique by the arm, and stopped. "Wait," he said. "Wait."

She was halfway through asking, "What is it?" when a second man, probably the store owner, came out carrying a shotgun. By now the first man was across the street and heading into an alley. The store owner didn't see this because he was running toward Digby and Veronique. Running and shouting, "Hey! I've been robbed! Which way did he go? Did you see him?"

Digby stepped in front of Veronique. "We didn't see anyone," he said.

"Aw, for Chrissake," said the owner. He was red in the face and breathing hard. "Look, I'll go one way, you go the other. He was a Mex, young. He's got a gun."

"No," said Digby. "I'm not a cop and we didn't see anything. We were talking."

The man got redder. "For Chrissake, what do you mean you're not a cop? What the hell kind of service is this? I pay taxes and..." He had been holding the shotgun upright but as he talked, he pumped his arms back and forth. Each time he did this, the barrel dipped low.

Assuming a voice he'd sometimes used in the Army when he was in the M.P.s, Digby said, "Let me see that weapon, mister." The man, caught off guard by the calm authority and probably himself a veteran, handed the shotgun to Digby, who promptly opened it and pulled out the shells, which he put in his pocket before handing the gun back.

"Let's go," Digby said to Veronique. As they turned and headed back to the set, the man started shouting again. "I'll report you. I've got your badge number. I'll report you."

After they'd gone a few yards, Veronique said, "I saw where the man went. He went across the street."

"No kidding?" said Digby.

"You saw him, too."

"You think so?" said Digby.

"Why didn't you tell him?"

"I've got a job," he said with a slight emphasis on "got".

The story went instantly around the set and from there to

the studio. That night, Lou told him he'd done a good job. The next day, he and Lou were called to Vogler's office. Digby had been at the studio for almost a year and had seen Vogler a number of times but they hadn't spoken since that conversation in the beach house, just a nod and sometimes a hello from the boss. Now Vogler said, "I heard how you handled yourself out there."

"There wasn't much to it," said Digby. "I didn't really do anything."

"That's the point, Digby, that's the point," said Vogler. "You didn't lose your head, go off half-cocked and do anything stupid. You never forgot who you're working for. I've been keeping an eye on you." He stood up behind his desk and extended his hand, so Digby got up and they shook and Vogler went on, "I'm glad you're with us."

"Thank you, sir," said Digby, "I'm glad to be here."

Vogler's intercom phone buzzed. He answered it, listened, then said, "In a minute." To Lou, he said, "Don't go," which Digby understood meant that his part of the meeting was over. He thanked Vogler again and left.

As he passed through Vogler's outer office on the way out, he saw George Marcus waiting to be sent in. The bookie had his hat in his hands and was turning it round and around, as though he was nervous or had something on his mind. He barely nodded to Digby.

Chapter 5

"Did you hear about the starlet who was so dumb she slept with writers?"

"That's a good one, Mr. Swink. Don't you want to come along home now?"

The writer was drunk. Lou had been sent to retrieve him from a bar near the studio and get him home. Shortly after Digby had distinguished himself on the *Dark Horizon* location, his pay had gone up and he began being taken along by Lou on off-the-lot missions like this one, out of uniform and in plain clothes.

Lou had been alerted to Swink's drinking himself stupid by the bartender, one of an extensive network which included maître ds, parking attendants and others who made it their business to know which celebrities belonged to which studio and who to call if there was trouble or the prospect of it. Swink, a writer, wouldn't usually rate this treatment, but, as Lou explained to Digby, he was a relative of Mrs. Vogler, a cousin or something.

Swink had another joke. "Did you hear about the writer who comes home and finds his wife in bed with his agent?" He interrupted himself when he recognized Digby. "Hi there. Good to see you," he said.

"Good to see you," said Digby.

"Glad to see you're getting up in the world," said Swink. He had been resisting Lou's efforts. Now Digby saw a way. "Say, Mr. Swink…"

"Don't you want to hear the rest of the joke?"

"I'm new at this," said Digby. "How about making me look good with the boss here by coming with us now?"

Swink considered this for a moment before answering, "Well, sure. But let me tell the joke first, then we'll go. Okay?"

"Fair enough," said Digby. Lou said nothing, curious to see how this was going to work out.

"So, as I was saying, a writer comes home to find his wife in bed with his agent. And he's stunned. He says, 'I can't believe it. My agent's come to my house.'"

Digby did his best to laugh, although he didn't really understand the joke.

"I guess I didn't tell it very well," said Swink.

As they drove Swink home, Digby asked about a matter that had come to mind a number of times since his last encounter with the writer. "Say, Mr. Swink, do you remember a while back you were working on that story about the twins, the detective and the criminal? Did you ever figure it out?"

"Yeah," said Swink. "It came to me one day. The cop doesn't have a twin. The twins are sisters. The cop's in love with the good one. And then we dropped the twins angle altogether. Just two sisters, one good the other bad."

"That's a long way from what you started with," said Digby. "How'd you think that up?"

"You try everything," said Swink.

As they pulled up in front of Swink's home, Digby said, "I'd like to see the movie. When's it coming out? What's it called?"

"*I Loved Them Both*," said Swink. "If you missed it, you're outta luck. It's come and gone. As a matter of fact, Digby, you know that French gal, Veronique, the one you helped out?

"Sure," said Digby.

"She did *I Loved Them Both* after *Dark Horizon*. It was the last of a three-picture deal she had. They've sent her back to France." He lowered his voice in mock theatricality. "Some people say it's because she wouldn't fuck Vogler, but you didn't get that from me."

"You want Digby to help you to the door?" asked Lou.

"Nah, I'll manage." He looked glumly out the window for

a few full seconds, then got out and started up the path to the house and Mrs. Swink.

As they drove away, Lou said to Digby, "You've got the touch, kid, I gotta say. You're good with people."

It wasn't long after this that Lou asked Digby if he had anything planned for the coming Sunday afternoon. Before Digby could answer, he went on to say, "Because if you do, cancel it. You're going to a party."

"Great," said Digby. "Where's the bash?"

"At the Voglers."

"Really?"

"Don't get excited," said Lou. "You're not going as a guest. You'll be working. You don't get paid extra. But you'll be remembered at Christmas."

"Okay," said Digby.

"It's easy duty. Just keep your eyes peeled. Someone gets really drunk, you might have to help them to the toilet. Break up any fights. And there's always the chance that someone who's not invited slips in. If you see someone dropping silverware into their pocket or something, don't do anything. Just let me know. Mingle, but don't socialize."

"What do I do if someone starts talking to me?" asked Digby.

"No one will," said Lou. "Don't worry about that. Everyone will know you're nobody."

"Oh, okay, then," said Digby.

The party wasn't at the Vogler beach house but at their place off Benedict Canyon, up behind the Beverly Hills Hotel, at the very top, at the end of a short private road. It looked to Digby like the house – what was it called, "Tara" ? – in *Gone With the Wind*, three stories in the Southern Plantation style, complete with broad columned portico. He felt like he was in a movie as he strode up the steps to the front door, a Yankee intruder.

Before he could knock, the door was opened by a man in a butler's tail coat.

"I'm Digby," he said. "From the studio."

"Lou's at the bar," said the butler, nodding down the entry hall, toward a huge sunken living room filled with easy chairs, couches, coffee tables, arranged in groups. Rather than thread his way through this to the bar, which was at the far end of the room, Digby worked his way around the perimeter, passing smaller rooms that opened off this one – a library lined with books, a room with a regulation-size billiard table, and a den, with a desk and a heavy-looking piece of furniture with a small screen set in it, a television, the first Digby had ever seen in someone's home. No one he knew owned one. The only television shows he'd ever seen even parts of, mainly professional wrestling, had been snatches on sets displayed in the windows of the hardware stores where they were sold.

When Digby finally got to the bar, Lou went over the instructions again. "Eyes open. Circulate but don't mingle. No booze." He turned to the bartender. "House special." The bartender poured something from a bottle out of sight into a tall glass and put it in front of Digby. It looked like whiskey.

"Iced tea," said Lou. "You have to have something in your hands."

After a while, as the sun set and the shadows outside grew long, guests began to arrive. The Voglers appeared. Waiters circulated with drinks and canapés.

Lou slid off his stool, saying to Digby, "Let's get to work."

It was, Digby realized, his first role. He had to pretend to be someone he wasn't, a guest. How should a guest act? He felt awkward and conspicuous. Surely he wasn't doing a very good job. It must be obvious to people that he wasn't who he was pretending to be. But Lou had been right earlier. No one paid any attention to him. Not for a while, anyway.

As he passed couples and small groups, he heard snatches

of conversations, talk of work, gossip, and laughter, much of it sincere. No wrongos here, as far as he could tell. At one point as he made his rounds, he passed Mr. Vogler, who nodded and gave him a slight, approving smile. Mrs. Vogler, with another small group, stopped him and told him how nice it was to see him again. It was the first time he had seen her since the night – was it three years ago? – that he had come ashore in Malibu. He thanked her for having been so kind to him then "and for all that's come of it."

"It's wonderful to see you doing well," she said.

He noticed a young woman, striking even in this crowd, lovely and fresh, different from almost everyone else in her bearing, her manner. What was it? She was, Digby realized, completely at ease as she chatted with an older couple, completely comfortable even though this was a place where everyone wanted to make a good impression. Then he realized he was looking at Cindy, the Vogler daughter, the girl who had fed him hot dogs that night, all grown up now. Even if she hadn't been Vogler's kid, what had given Kenny the idea he had any chance with her? He guessed that Kenny, being Kenny, just had to try. He probably wouldn't be the last guy to get in trouble over her.

And then he saw Betsy. *Goddamnit.* He'd been trying to forget about her, had made it to the point where a day might go by without his thinking about their time together. She was with an older man, Cy Sandler, a producer. She saw him, raised a hand in greeting. He managed a tight smile and turned away. Nothing requiring his professional attention happened during the rest of the evening but if someone had walked off with a couch he wouldn't have noticed.

He was brooding over a beer at his apartment after the party when Betsy called. "You weren't very friendly," she said.

He told her he had been working. "I wasn't a guest. I

wasn't supposed to mingle."

"Oh," said Betsy. Then she said she wanted to see him. She missed him. She hadn't realized how much she'd missed him until that evening.

Digby knew he shouldn't say, "Me, too," but he did. Then he said he'd be over to pick her up.

Chapter 6

Just because a picture is in the planning stages doesn't mean it will get made. This was the case with the John Payne comedy that was supposed to be Betsy's big break. She was, however, still able to hold on to the place on Spaulding in Beverly Hills, and Cy Sandler held on to her. Her time with Digby became furtive. Some men might have found this heightened the allure; it depressed Digby. He had to admit that something was happening he would have once thought impossible. He was beginning to lose interest. He was relieved that she almost never stayed overnight anymore.

He was alone the night the phone brought him out of a sleep so deep that he lay paralyzed for a few moments even after he was awake. When he was finally able to get his hand on the receiver and lift it to his ear, it was to hear Lou telling him to get his ass over to the all-night newsstand on Las Palmas.

"Right now," said Lou. "Jumping Jack is on the loose again."

"Meet you there," said Digby.

"No," said Lou. "You handle it yourself. It's time you start flying on your own. You know what to do, don't you?"

"Sure," said Digby, "I'm on it." This was his first solo assignment. He wondered if it meant a raise was in the near future.

Within a few minutes he was dressed and on his way. Jack Scott was a valuable asset to the studio. It was crucial to get to him before he tried to pick up an undercover vice-squad cop. The police in the smaller towns – Culver City, Santa Monica, Burbank – were manageable; in Beverly Hills they were positively courtly in their treatment of misbehaving celebrities. The L.A. cops could be real pricks, and of course

41

Hollywood Boulevard was smack in the middle of their juris-diction.

He pulled up at the Las Palmas News Stand, a wall of newspapers, tout sheets and magazines nearly half a block long, lit bright as day. Joey, the night manager, hopped off his stool by the register with surprising agility given his enormous girth, and came over for his twenty dollars for having called Lou about Scott.

Digby handed him the money and asked, "Where is he? At church, I suppose," nodding down the block towards the Baptist Church of Hollywood, which by some quirk of city planning had few street lamps near it and therefore sat in a patch of deep shadow. Its steps were well established as a place for men who wanted to meet men.

"Nope," said Joey. "He came up from there. Guess he couldn't find anyone. Hung around here for a while. That's when I called Lou. Then he headed up thataway." He pointed up the street, toward Hollywood Boulevard. "Turned left at the corner."

"Okay, thanks."

"You can't miss her," said Joey. "She's the broad in the purple dress with the five o'clock shadow." Joey could be quite the wit.

"Great," said Digby. "That's just great." He pulled away from the curb and found a parking spot. This was a job to be done on foot. He'd have to look in every bar and coffee shop, every dark doorway, every alley.

He got to the Boulevard, glanced in the window of a short-order place and got lucky. There, showing himself off to the world from a window seat, was his quarry, Jumping Jack Scott, star of the studio's about-to-be-released *Frontier Gunman*. In a dress. Fortunately, he was also wearing a wig, a hat and makeup, so there was some chance he wouldn't be recognized. Digby hurried in.

As he approached Scott, the actor flashed an inviting smile which disappeared as Digby got closer. "Oh, it's you," he said.

Even though this wasn't Digby's first time retrieving Scott under these circumstances it was still strange to hear that well-known, thoroughly masculine drawl coming out of that face with its lipstick, powder and mascara. Some of the powder was flaking off. Joey was right abuot the five o'clock shadow.

"Yes, sir," said Digby. "Your ride home."

"What if I'm not ready to go home?"

"Well," said Digby, "I can't force you."

"Right enough," said Scott. "You can't."

"But," Digby continued, "I can stay with you. You know how it goes. Everywhere you go, I'll go. You go down the street, I'll be with you. You go up the street, me. You go into a bar, I'll be right with you. So you probably won't have much luck meeting anyone. So you might as well let me take you home."

Scott's lips pursed slightly and his brow furrowed. Even with the makeup, Digby recognized that look, the look that audiences loved, as Scott was making up his mind to take on an outlaw band singlehandedly or run his PT boat at an approaching Japanese battleship. Now it was, "Should I or shouldn't I call it a night?"

Scott milked the moment, as he so often did on screen. On the screen, he always chose the heroic action, but it seemed that in real life he could take the wiser course. He said, "Well, I've got an early call tomorrow," pulled out a bill for the check and stood up.

"We'll take your car," said Digby. "You don't want to leave it around here overnight."

"We? I'm okay to drive," said Scott. He wobbled slightly as he walked, probably as much because of the heels he was wearing as from a load of liquor but Digby didn't want him driving. He knew better than to push this man any further and so resorted to a variation of his "let me look good to my boss" tactic. "Please," he said, "I'll lose my job if anything goes wrong. Let me drive you home. That's the way I want to be able to tell it to my boss."

Jack Scott was nothing if not understanding of the common man. "Okay, then," he said, "let's hit the trail," and handed Digby the keys.

The actor owned a sprawling ranch house way out at the far end of the Valley. Fortunately, though, when he was shooting at the studio, as he was at the moment, he stayed at a much smaller, elegant little place he had on Whitley Heights, half a mile up the hill from the Boulevard. When they got there, Digby pulled the car into the driveway and switched off the ignition.

Neither man had said much during the drive but now, suddenly, in the moment before they got out of the car, Scott asked Digby, "Do I disgust you?"

"No," said Digby. That was true. But he was puzzled. Apparently this was evident to Scott. The star said, "Something's on your mind. Come on, spit it out, Lieutenant."

It seemed to Digby that "spit out it, Lieutenant" was a line from one of Scott's movies. Something set in the Civil War. Or maybe...actually, he thought it turned up in more than one of his pictures.

"Well, I'm waiting..." said Scott. Another one of his signature lines.

"To tell you the truth," said Digby, "I wonder why you do it. I mean, you're taking an awful chance when you go out like this."

"Maybe I like taking chances," said Scott. Digby didn't remember that from any of his movies. Then, with a strange half smile Digby was sure the star had never used on-camera, he added, "It spices things up, taking chances. It gives me a kick."

After they were out of the car and Digby had given him back his keys, Scott said, "Come on in. I'll call you a cab."

"No, it's okay," said Digby. "It's not far. It's downhill. I'll leg it."

"Sure?"

"Sure," said Digby. He waved goodnight as Scott let himself into the house, walked half a block and waited. Five minutes. Ten. He went back up. The car was still in the driveway.

When he got home, about half an hour later and called Lou to let him know all was well, he got a busy signal, which probably meant that Lou had taken the phone off the hook so he could sleep undisturbed for the rest of the night.

Despite his promotion and occasional off-the-lot assignments, Digby still had routine duties. At about ten the next morning, he was making his rounds when Lou's voice squawked from his walkie-talkie, telling him to come to the office.

"What happened with Scott last night? You found him? Was there any trouble?"

"No," said Digby. "I found him. Took him home."

"Got him in the house?"

"I saw him go in and I checked a little later. What's wrong?"

"He hasn't turned up," said Lou. "He was due on Stage 6 an hour and a half ago. No one's answering the phone. They sent someone up there. No one answered the door. You better go find out if he's out cold or something."

When Digby pulled up outside Scott's house, he was relieved to see that the car seemed to still be exactly where he had parked it.

He went to the front door, pushed the bell, heard a chime inside the house. No one answered. Shouldn't there be a houseman or a maid or someone around? He rang again.

He went up the driveway, around the back of the house, knocked at the back door and called out. Nothing.

He found a window, which was locked shut, tried another, which wasn't and climbed through into a narrow pantry. He called out a couple of times, "Hello, hello," as he made his way across the kitchen and through a door which led into the dining room. Everything was still and quiet. Sunlight streamed through a stained-glass window.

He moved from the dining room into the entryway and there, sprawled out on the tile floor at the foot of the stairs, was Jack Scott. Still wearing his dress. "Oh, shit," said Digby.

Scott was flat on his back, his arms spread wide, his head turned slightly to one side. His eyes were closed, his mouth half open as though stopped in the middle of a yawn. His hat, a silly little pink beret, lay a few inches from his head.

When Digby was in in the M.P.s, he had handled men unconscious from drinking or fighting or both, and he'd handled men who were dead. Scott was dead. He took a deep breath to steady himself, then found the phone. When he got Lou, he said, "Something's happened to Scott."

"What?" asked Lou. "What's going on up there?"

"He's dead."

"Whaddya mean, he's dead? What the hell happened?"

"I don't know," said Digby. He explained about Scott lying at the foot of the stairs.

"What's he wearing?" asked Lou. "How is he dressed?"

"Just the way he was last night," said Digby. "Dress, all the stuff."

"Have you called the police?"

"I thought Id better call you first."

"Okay, good, good," said Lou. "Sit tight. Don't call anyone. I'm coming up."

Digby didn't like being in the room with the dead man so

he opened the front door, went out and sat on the front steps. Then, realizing that was not a particularly good idea – no point in attracting the attention of neighbors – he went back inside and sat in the dining room. Everything was just as it had been when he came in. Quiet, the sunlight streaming through the window, but of course now everything was different.

Lou was quick to arrive. When he saw Scott, he said, "Geeze, Louise, what a mess. I guess he must have lost his balance or something and fell down the stairs. Hit his head. That'll do it. How drunk was he?"

"Not bad. He seemed all right."

Lou got on the phone and called Vogler. After he explained the situation, he listened for a while, a couple of times saying, "Yes" and a couple of times, "No." When he got off the phone, he said to Digby, "Okay, let's do what we have to do here."

"Which is what?"

"They photograph corpses," said Lou as he turned Scott on his side so he could get at the zipper at the back of his dress. "Come on," he said to Digby, "give me a hand here." They wrestled the dress off, revealing the corset with chest pads to give Scott breasts. Digby was suddenly sickened by this parody of a woman's body. He hated being here. He thought of Betsy. That lovely flesh.

"That's a break," said Lou when they discovered that Scott was wearing jockey shorts rather than panties they would have to remove. He gathered up the clothes and the shoes and the hat, and headed up the stairs, leaving Digby standing by the body.

"Where you going?"

"Just wait a minute," said Lou.

What the hell is he doing up there? thought Digby. *He's taking a hell of a long time.*

When Lou did come back down, he was carrying a small

towel and a jar of cold cream. He bent down by Scott, opened the cream, dipped his fingers into it, and smeared some onto Scott's lips and face.

"Haven't you ever watched a dame do this?" As Lou wiped the makeup away, Digby was impressed by how efficiently, how calmly he was handling everything. It was almost as though he was prepared for this. Had he dealt with a situation like this before?

Lou stepped back, examining his handiwork. "That's not bad, not too bad." He bent back down, daubing here and there at the last of the makeup. "He'll look all right."

"What did you do with his clothes?" asked Digby.

"In the laundry basket. The cops'll find it and he's probably got a closet full of that stuff. There's nothing to be done about that."

Then he told Digby how it was going to be. "Here's what happened. Scott didn't show up for work this morning. You came up here, just the way you did. Door was locked, no answer, all that. You climbed in the back. You found him lying here. No drag, of course. You moved the body around. That's important. The cops will know he's been moved, so you tell them you moved him because you didn't know if he was dead or just out. You shook him, you shook him around. You pumped his chest. Lifeguard stuff. Then you called me. I told you to call the cops. I got here a few minutes before they did. Got it? Just the way it was except no drag and you moved the body around a little."

Digby didn't like being tagged with moving Scott but he reckoned it was best to rely on Lou. He did have a question. "What about last night?"

"Tell'em. In fact, tell them even if they don't ask. They know about Scott and they'll be down on the Boulevard asking around so they'll find out he was down there. But that's okay. We just don't want any pictures circulating of our boy in a dress. That's the word from up top. "

There were no sirens, just a squad car pulling up about fifteen minutes after Digby made the call. Two uniforms. "Wow," said one of the cops. "That's Jack Scott all right. What a shame." He didn't ask any questions and explained that detectives were on their way. A few minutes later, a second, unmarked car arrived.

Both of the detectives knew Lou. No one got excited. The older one of the two, who Lou addressed both as Lieutenant and as Jimmy, looked the body over carefully, then nodded to his partner, a sergeant named Ray, who got on the phone and started making calls.

The lieutenant wanted to know who had found Scott.

Digby explained about being sent over from the studio when Scott didn't turn up for work, everything just as Lou had instructed.

"You shouldn't have moved the body," said the lieutenant.

"I was trying to help him. I didn't know…"

"Anyone else around here?" asked the lieutenant. "Doesn't he have anyone, any staff up here? A cook or something?"

"Haven't seen anyone," said Digby.

The lieutenant returned to the subject of Scott's corpse. "I want to hear what the coroner has to say, of course, but I'd guess he's been dead for about ten hours, so whatever happened, happened about one a.m."

That startled Digby. He hadn't thought about it, but he realized now that he was probably the last person to see Scott alive.

Lou spoke up, "Digby brought Scott home last night. I got a call he was prowling around places he shouldn't be, so I sent Digby to round him up."

Digby took the cue and told his story.

"You didn't bring him into the house?" asked the lieutenant.

"No," said Digby, "the last I saw of him, he was letting himself in."

"And he was just in his underwear I suppose?"

Digby said nothing. The lieutenant continued, "Okay, so he came into the house, went upstairs, took off whatever he was dressed up in and then somehow fell down the stairs." He didn't say this as though he believed it.

"I don't know what happened after he went in the house."

A hearse marked "Coroner" arrived, followed shortly by a car bringing a photographer and a fingerprint man. The photographer shot the body, the coroner looked it over, then he and the sergeant covered it and took it out to the hearse.

When the sergeant returned, he and the lieutenant began slowly going up the stairway, examining each step, the bannister and the wall. The photographer followed, shooting details the detectives pointed out to him, followed by the fingerprint man, who dusted, looking for prints and finding a few.

Digby and Lou seemed to have been forgotten. When Lou asked if they could go back to the studio, the lieutenant said, "Sure. Go ahead." To Digby he said, "We may be speaking again."

They were on their way out the door when more cars pulled up, carrying the press. The uniformed cops wouldn't let any of them in the house. Then, just as Lou and Digby, refusing to answer any questions, made it back to their cars, one more car arrived, driven by a middle-aged Filipino man who jumped out and came across the front lawn, taking it all in.

"Hey, Fernando," said Lou.

"What's happened? What's happened?"

"There's been an accident," said Lou.

"Is Mr. Jack all right?"

"Fernando," said Lou, "he's dead."

"Oh, my God, my God," said Fernando. He ran for the house.

Lou said to Digby, "That's Scott's houseman. I guess it was his night off."

A little later, when they were back in Lou's office, Digby asked what kind of trouble they might be in.

"No one's in trouble," said Lou.

"I mean, for undressing Scott."

"They can't prove that. They probably suspect it but they can't prove it. They're going to decide that Scott was drunk and, in drag or not, fell down the stairs. It happens. End of story, end of investigation." But when he sat down behind his desk, he sagged into the chair and said he might knock off early and go home. He asked Digby how he was doing.

"I'm okay." In fact, he felt nervy, exhausted and steamed up at the same time, like a man who's been up so long he can't sleep. "Maybe I'll take a break, if that's okay. Get lunch off the lot."

"Sure," said Lou.

He called Betsy. She was busy, she had things planned. "I've got places I'm expected. I can't just come running…"

He interrupted. "It's been a hell of a morning," he said, and was relieved, pleased, when she cared enough to ask, "Are you all right?"

"I'll tell you about it when I see you. Come on. I need you."

"Okay," she said, "okay."

On the way to pick her up, he stopped to get a couple of sandwiches and some beer, so by the time he got to her apartment, Betsy had already heard that Scott was dead. "It was on the radio," she said. "Does this have anything to do with that?" she asked.

"It does."

"So what happened? They said they don't know. 'Details not released' or something. Are you mixed up in that?"

He snapped at her when he said, "I'm not 'mixed up' in anything," apologized, and went on tell her what had happened, the version he'd given the police.

"So you found the body," she said. "I guess that was not very nice."

"No, it wasn't," he said. He moved closer to her.

"Do you think there's going to be a scandal?" She didn't seemed pleased by the prospect.

Digby wished she'd stop talking. "I'm glad you're here," he said.

It was hours later, while they were napping, that his doorbell rang. By the time he got to the door, his visitor was knocking.

It was the sergeant. He said the lieutenant wanted to see him and would appreciate it very much if he would come downtown with him.

"Now?" asked Digby. "He wants me right now?"

"Yes. Now. If you could. He'd appreciate it." There was no irony in the request.

"Well, okay, sure," said Digby. "Give me a minute." He turned to go to the bedroom. When the sergeant tried to come in, Digby blocked his way. "I'll be just a minute," he said, closed the door and went to tell Betsy he'd be back as soon as he could.

At the station, the sergeant led him to a small room. "The lieutenant will be along," he said and left Digby there, sitting by himself at a bare table. Nothing happened. After some time, the door opened again. It still wasn't the lieutenant. "He's tied up. He'll be along," said the sergeant. "Do you want some coffee?"

"Yes, sure, coffee."

The door closed again. Digby wondered if this was some tactic, to wear him down and make him worry so that he would lose his bearings and say or do something stupid. What was this about, anyway? Lou had said there wouldn't be a fuss about the way they'd handled the body. He was suddenly in mind of that time, a few years back, when he'd been caught by the current that had carried him out to sea and how important it had been to stay calm. It had happened again, in a way, when he'd found Scott's body. He had been caught by a great force which threatened to pull him into dangerous waters. He got up to open the door to let them know he wasn't rattled, had nothing to be rattled about, planning to tell the cop to make his coffee black. The knob wouldn't turn. The door was locked.

He looked at his watch. About ten minutes later, the lieutenant came in, carrying a paper cup.

"Hello, Digby."

"Hello, Lieutenant." He had a feeling he'd seen a situation like this in some movie. At least one. Was it with Bogart? Maybe Dick Powell. He felt confident. He could handle this. "Is that my coffee?" he asked.

"No," said the lieutenant. "Did you want some?"

"It's okay," said Digby. "Never mind."

"How do you take it? Black, cream? Sugar?"

"Forget it," said Digby. "It's okay."

"No, if you want some coffee…"

"I'm fine," said Digby. "I'm fine."

"Okay, good" said the lieutenant. "I'll tell you quite frankly why you're here. I wanted to talk to you privately, away from the people you work for. You understand, don't you, even the studio can only help you up to a point."

"Help me with what?" asked Digby. He tried to keep his tone neutral. No fear, no irritation. Calm.

The lieutenant went on. "The way it works, me, the D.A. everyone concerned really appreciates cooperation. You know how it is. Someone makes your job a little easier, shows you respect by telling you the truth, you appreciate that and try to reciprocate. Do you see what I'm saying?"

"I'm not sure that I do," said Digby. He said it as respectfully as he could.

"If you tell us right now what happened... There'll be an autopsy, and the evidence team is still working on Scott's place. If they, I mean the coroner or the on-site boys, turn up anything, it's better if you've cooperated."

"I am cooperating, Lieutenant. Really."

"We know all about Jack Scott," said the Lieutenant, "so I don't blame you. No one will blame you. But we have to know what happened."

"What happened is what I've already told you. I got Scott off the Boulevard, took him home, saw him go into his house and the next time I saw him, he was lying there on the floor in his hallway."

"On his face or on his back?"

"His back."

"So you dropped him off, he went upstairs, got out of his outfit, decided to go downstairs for some reason. Maybe to get a sandwich..."

"Yes, could be," said Digby.

"And," continued the Lieutenant, "he was drunk, missed his step, and fell down the stairs?"

"Yeah," said Digby.

"Did he try to walk down the stairs backwards?"

"I doubt it."

"So how did he wind up on his back?"

The lieutenant, he had to admit, had a point. "Maybe," said Digby, "he slipped on his way back up?"

"From getting his snack in the kitchen?"

"Could be."

"So where's the snack? Not on the stairs. Nothing in the kitchen. How about this? You didn't leave him at the door. You came inside with him. I'm not saying you wanted to, but he made some excuse. Got you inside, got you to come upstairs Then he tried to get you to go along with what he likes. You pushed him away and that's how it happened."

Holy Christ! They think I killed Scott. "No, no, Lieutenant, I swear. You're making up a story that didn't happen."

"It would explain everything," said the Lieutenant.

"Except that it's not true," said Digby.

The lieutenant shook his head in a manner meant to signify sorrow. "I wish you'd come to your senses, Digby. If they find your prints upstairs or the coroner finds some evidence Scott was punched, you'll wish you'd made a deal when you had a chance."

"I don't have to make any deals," said Digby. "I didn't do anything."

"Think it over."

"Are you holding me?"

"I'll get your coffee, give you a little time" said the lieutenant.

Digby decided that meant they weren't arresting him. "I don't need any time," he said. "I'd like to go now. Can someone take me or should I call a cab?"

"You're just going to walk out of here without helping us or yourself, is that it?"

"I've told you everything I know, Lieutenant."

The lieutenant gave him a long, appraising look, then shrugged and said, "I'll get someone to take you."

Digby hoped Betsy would be waiting for him. Maybe there was some way they could get back to the way things had been before, but when he got home she was gone.

Chapter 7

The next day, at work, when Digby told Lou about his interview with the lieutenant, Lou said, "They're just checking out all the possibilities, and let's face it, you're one of them."

"Jesus," said Digby.

"I mean, as far as they're concerned," said Lou.

"You think they really do suspect me, what the lieutenant said, that I got in a fight with him?"

"You've got nothing to worry about. Unless, of course..."

"Unless what? That's not so funny," said Digby. "You really think I might do something like that?"

"You're the only one who knows that for a fact, aren't you?" said Lou. His smile got broader.

"Jesus!"

"Oh, keep your shirt on, Digby. I'm just giving you the rib."

When other people on the lot asked him about the case, Digby said he wasn't supposed to talk about it, and changed the subject.

The legitimate newspapers, like the *Times* and the *News*, didn't have enough to work the story for more than a couple of days. Louella and Hedda, in their respective columns, spoke of a "freak accident" and "great loss to the industry and his fans." The scandal sheets ran big headlines and dropped dark hints but even they couldn't squeeze much out of it.

Digby kept track of the investigation through Lou, who kept in touch with the lieutenant. Nothing appeared to have been stolen from Scott's house. Fernando, the houseman, had a son who worked at Scott's ranch and sometimes came and went from the Hollywood house on errands but he had an alibi for that night, as, for that matter, did Fernando. No one in the homosexual community had picked up any gossip about trouble with a trick.

"The cops can keep it as an open case," Lou explained to Digby, "which they hate to do and do only if there's definitely been a crime, or they can declare it an accident and get it off their desks. I think you can forget about it."

Despite Lou's assurances, the matter remained on Digby's mind. Would he be hearing from the police again, what exactly had happened to Scott? He wanted an end to it even as the ordinary course of things resumed. Mrs. Vogler had taken up the cause of a local orchestra. A group of players from it would be the centerpiece of a Sunday afternoon affair at the house. He and Lou would be working the affair.

When he got to the house, he wasn't at all surprised to find his boss and a few of the household staff standing just outside the den, where the Voglers were watching television along with a few early guests. Everyone was following the drama of little Kathy Fiscus, unfolding in a field just east of downtown.

Two days earlier, on Friday afternoon, Kathy, three and a half years old, was playing near her home when she ran through a patch of weeds covering the rotted wooden cover of an abandoned water well. The wood gave way. Little Kathy plunged into the shaft, becoming wedged about a hundred feet down.

Police and fire units came quickly. Kathy was crying. She was alive. Her parents called down to her. "Don't worry. We'll get you out." Shortly afterwards, the crying stopped. A doctor called to the scene speculated that she had slipped into a coma which, by slowing her metabolism, might actually improve her chance of survival, but how long could she last?

The initial plan for getting her out was to lower a rescuer who would pull her free and then be winched back to the surface. When the shaft proved too narrow for a man of ordinary size, there was talk of calling Santa Anita or

Hollywood Park for a jockey, but even a jockey might be too big. How about a midget? Preferably one with acrobatic skills, since he would have to lowered upside down. Where to find someone like that? The roster at the Screen Actors Guild was consulted, several small men dispatched. Even they, however, couldn't manage it.

Kathy would have to be dug out. The field filled with trucks, bulldozers, drilling equipment, ready to work round the clock. Lighting would be needed, lots of it, so another call went out to Hollywood. The Vogler studio was among those sending the generators and lamps used on movie sets.

Newspaper reporters appeared, then a rig for on-the-spot radio coverage, soon followed by newsreel men with their cameras. The photographs of all this that appeared in the papers reminded Digby of the location shoot for *Dark Horizon*, as though someone was making a movie about the rescue of a child.

And then something new had appeared on the field where the desperate story was playing out – a pair of vans from a local television station, providing live, continuous visual coverage, a first in the history of broadcasting.

As Digby joined Lou and the others watching the TV from outside the den, the on-camera reporter was handed a bulletin which only repeated all the earlier bulletins – crews were getting closer to little Kathy. Was she still alive? "We all hope so," said the announcer.

The Vogler butler came up, watched for a moment, then said, quietly, "Let's go, folks." Cars were pulling up. More guests were arriving, some familiar to Digby, others new to him, probably the serious music crowd.

Alan Swink and his wife came through the door.

"Hey, there, Digby. You into this long hair stuff?"

"I don't know much about it, Mr. Swink."

"I'm more of a Benny Goodman man myself. My wife just

brings me along to keep her company."

"I'm not really here for the music," said Digby. "I'm working."

"Oh, yeah. Gotchya," said Swink. "Say, listen, anything new on Jack Scott?"

"Nothing, Mr. Swink. I think it's pretty much a closed matter. Nice seeing you. I'm supposed to circulate."

"Okay, then. Carry on."

The furniture had been rearranged so that all the chairs and couches faced a raftered platform set up at one end of the room. Now, a man's voice called out, asking everyone to take a seat. As people settled down, Mrs. Vogler spoke, welcoming her guests and then introducing the players as they took their places. Just strings. No piano, let alone drums or horns. It didn't look to Digby as though this was going to be much fun.

He found the first few pieces cheerful enough; the rest seemed dreary. Even so, he recognized vaguely, without being able to follow it all, that there was structure here, development and variation in each piece, with nothing introduced that wasn't accounted for at the end and resolved.

Some of the crowd seemed genuinely moved; some seemed to just be sitting it out.

After the performance and the applause, the random noises of the room resumed, the conversations, the occasional exclamation rising above the general tone. Suddenly a stir passed through, a wave of excitement that was almost palpable. "They've found Kathy. They've got down to where she is."

The crowd headed for the television in the den, far more than the room could accommodate. A man near the set called out. "They're bringing her up."

Lou signaled to Digby and they, together with a couple of the Vogler house staff, squeezed into the den. The plan was to move the set out into the living room. They had an extension cord but they were stymied when they realized that the set had to remain attached to the antenna wire. There was no way to extend that. It was in the middle of this confusion and distraction that the announcer looked into the camera and said, "I'm afraid she didn't make it. Little Kathy Fiscus is gone from us."

"What? What happened?" people outside the room asked. As the news spread, people fell silent. Soon the party was breaking up, people leaving, the valets getting their cars.

Digby found himself near the front door. Two couples, one of them Alan Swink and his wife, were standing together, waiting for their cars, the other man saying to Swink, "Well, there's a picture in it."

"You think so?" asked Swink.

"You kidding? Kid trapped in a well... Someone'll do it."

"Yeah" said Swink, "but they get the kid out alive and okay."

"Yeah, sure, of course."

"You need something more," said Swink.

"Did you know the kid's father worked for the company that drilled the well?"

"That so?" asked Swink. "Is that a fact?"

"Now, I have to say they drilled it and covered it up long before he came to work for them. Years ago. It's an old well."

"Oh..."

"But get this," said the man, "the day before the kid fell in, her father was in Sacramento testifying to some commission that there ought to be a law that all old wells have to be sealed with cement, and then he comes back to L.A. and this happens. Which, if you think about it, is great because if he was a villain, you know, saying it would cost too much or be too hard to find and seal all the wells and then his kid falls in, that would be too obvious, too pat and on the nose."

"You know," said Swink, "either way, I don't know, it's too perfect. It's phony. The audience wouldn't believe it."

"But it's true," said the other man.

"So," said Swink, "you're saying do a version of the story with a happy ending. They get the kid out, but leave in the true stuff about her father trying to convince the state to seal all the wells before she falls in."

"Yeah," said the other man. "Happy ending. Absolutely. You'd have to wait a year or so until people forget exactly what happened but then you could do it with a happy ending."

The other man's wife spoke up. "No matter when you do it, even in a year, people will remember this. They'll remember what really happened, that they couldn't save Kathy and it'll be depressing."

"Yeah…yeah," said her husband, not mocking her but conceding the rightness of her position. Swink nodded his agreement.

Their cars arrived, and just as the couples parted, Swink said, "But Glenn Ford for the father."

Chapter 8

Driving home, Digby had to slam on his brakes when he caught himself about to run a red light, distracted by a turmoil of despair and confusion. Things happened to people. They fell down stairs, they fell down wells. Random death; and mixed in with this was concern about his own situation, things hanging with Betsy, and of course the always-present possibility that the cops would be back at him about Scott.

He was passing a theater on La Brea. On impulse, without looking at the marquee to see what was playing, he went in, found a seat, slumped down and tried to lose himself in the picture, which was already underway. It was a melodrama, a triangle with complications and a couple of twists which Digby had trouble following, but he had come in in the middle and he was distracted. The rest of the audience seemed satisfied by how it all wrapped up and finished.

That night, just after he got into bed, it came to him in a frenzy, a flood of questions he hadn't allowed himself to ask, and answers. Yes, there was more to Scott's death. Why had Lou chosen that particular night to send him out on his first solo round-up of the star? Why had the phone been busy when he tried to report back? Suppose Lou had taken the phone off the hook because he didn't want Digby to know he had in fact gone out after calling him? Suppose that while Digby was down on the Boulevard catching up with Scott, Lou had broken into Scott's house and gone upstairs to wait for him. But why? Suppose he wanted to intimidate Scott about something, demonstrate how easy it was for someone to get to him? Was it a coincidence that Fernando the houseman was off for the night? That was something Lou might very well know about.

Why would Lou want to put the arm on Scott? That was

easy. It could involve someone else Digby knew, George Marcus, the bookie. After all, Scott was a man who got a kick out of taking chances. Maybe he played the horses and owed Marcus a lot of money and was slow to pay up. Maybe Lou was collecting for Marcus. Maybe Mr. Vogler himself was involved. Digby had seen Marcus in Vogler's office. Suppose Vogler was concerned that Scott was coming dangerously close to getting roughed up by goons working for Marcus. A broken leg or slashed face would disrupt the studio's schedule. Maybe Vogler had gotten Lou to demonstrate Scott's vulnerability to him so that he would square things with Marcus. The Lou who had scared Kenny out of town was certainly capable of that. For whatever reason, Lou could have been there and there could have been a confrontation, a fight that ended with Scott's fall. And with the way it had been arranged afterwards, if anyone had to be blamed, it was Digby who'd been put on the spot.

Or was he just spinning his wheels, creating connections where they didn't exist? If he could get all of it out of his head somehow and examine it…maybe by telling it to someone.

On Monday, at the studio, he found himself outside the Writers Building, by the fountain and the drooping weeping willow, debating whether to follow through with his plan when the man he was thinking of visiting, Alan Swink, came up behind him. Digby asked if he could spare a few minutes.

"Have I been parking my car in the wrong space?"

"Nothing like that. To tell you the truth…" He hesitated to say it.

"What is it, Digby?" Swink smiled, making a joke off it. "Out with it, man."

Dingy plunged on. "You know about stories, about telling stories."

"It's how I earn my daily bread," said Swink.

"I want to get your opinion about something…a story that's

on my mind."

Swink looked dubious. "I've got a typist waiting for me."

"It's kind of a murder mystery."

This interested Swink. "It wouldn't have anything to do with Scott, would it?"

"Sort of, in a way, yes."

Swink invited Digby up to his office, got the typist going, then settled down behind his desk, Digby across from him. "Shoot," he said. "Whattaya got?"

Digby started slowly, then it began to spill out of him almost faster than he could talk.

"Whoa, whoa," said Swink. "Slow down. First, you're making all this up, right? You don't know if any of this about Lou or George is true?"

"No," said Digby. "It's just ideas about it."

"It's pretty complicated. Too complicated Too many what-ifs and maybes. Do the cops think you did something?"

"I guess not," said Digby. "They haven't been around for a month now."

"Are they acting like it's a crime at all instead of just an accident?"

"Not that I know of, to tell the truth."

"So why is it still on your mind?"

Digby didn't really know. He was trying to explain it to himself as much as to Swink when he said, "It's just... Once you start thinking about it, there are so many possibilities. Why do things happen the way they do? And the people you think you know, who are they really? Why do they do what they do?"

Swink lit a cigarette, drew deeply on it, studied the cloud of smoke he exhaled, and then said, "Digby, what you want is the consolation of literature, the ragged edge of life sewn up."

"You think so?"

"I'll tell you, though, you might be on to something. We

couldn't set it in a studio, though."

What was Swink talking about? Well, yes, of course. It was second nature with these guys to try to turn things into movies.

Swink was going on, "For some reason, movies about the movies are poison at the box office. We'll have to set it some place else. Maybe Broadway. Or maybe some big factory. A loyal underling discovers that his boss committed a murder or ordered one, and they're setting him up to take the fall for it. Of course, he turns the tables on them and comes out the winner." He was clearly warming to the possibilities. "And he's got a girl. There's a moment when she doubts him, or he thinks she does, but she sticks with him, through and through."

Digby thought of Betsy.

"Tell you what," said Swink, "let me work it up, see what I can come up with. What magic I can weave. If they go for it, I'll get some story money for you. What do you say?"

"I guess. Sure."

"You've never written a screenplay, right?"

"True."

"So you won't be in on that. But if I can make it happen, you'll get some dough. And a credit. Who knows what could come of it, Digby, who knows? I've seen people go far with less."

The typist came into the room. She couldn't read a change Swink had scribbled on a page.

"All right," said Swink to Digby. "Let me noodle on it. I'll let you know. We may have something."

Back in his patrol cart, continuing his rounds, Digby felt relieved, lightened, for having laid it all out. His version of things really was unlikely when you considered it. He much preferred the way Swink told it. And he liked the idea that he might make some money. He wondered how much…but considering this point led to another thought. Would Vogler or Lou get sore when they heard what Swink was selling? Would they realize what – who – had inspired it? What would happen then? And would that fit into Swink's version or be part of some other story?

At Roundfire we publish great stories. We lean towards the spiritual and thought-provoking. But whether it's literary or popular, a gentle tale or a pulsating thriller, the connecting theme in all Roundfire fiction titles is that once you pick them up you won't want to put them down.

Also from Roundfire

Getting Right

(9781785351891) by Gary D. Wilson

Suppose your more than mildly irritating leech of a sister calls you, as she usually does wanting money, only this time she says instead that she has cancer and in the course of the conversation challenges you to write the story of her life. You say, sure, you'll do that but you'll tell it the way you see it.

The tale that emerges involves not only the dying sister, Connie, but brother Len as well. And it's also about "me," the sibling invited to narrate their shared story and whose interplay of memory and imagination raises the question of whether "the truth" of Connie's life–or of anyone's for that matter–can ever be known.

Oreads

(9781785351839) by John F. Lavelle

At fourteen Cassie Wolphe's way of life in Appalachia is being changed by the influx of modernity/postmodernity. She is in love with Jake McCollum, believes she will marry him and constructs her life around this central act, but like her brother, Ben, Jake rejects a life he believes offers nothing but hard work and poverty and forces Cassie to make a decision to either leave the mountains or split up. Although she loves Jake, she cannot leave the mountains. And so Cassie's personal journey into harsh reality begins...